THE HAUNTED HOUSE

THE HAUNTED HOUSE

A COLLECTION OF ORIGINAL STORIES

EDITED BY JANE YOLEN AND MARTIN H. GREENBERG

ILLUSTRATED BY DORON BEN-AMI

HarperCollins*Publishers*

FOR DANIEL HOWARD, WHO LIVES NEXT DOOR
—J.Y.

The Haunted House
A Collection of Original Stories
Copyright © 1995 by Jane Yolen and Martin H. Greenberg
"Somewhere a Puppy Cries" © 1995 by Mary K. Whittington
"The Paperdoll Ghost" © 1995 by Anna Grossnickle Hines
"Biscuits of Glory" © 1995 by Bruce Coville
"The Gourmet Ghost" © 1995 by Janet Gill-Lonergan
"And the Lights Flickered" © 1995 by Barbara Diamond Goldin
"Night Wolves" © 1995 by Jane Yolen
"The Train Room" © 1995 by Gary Hines

Library of Congress Cataloging-in-Publication Data
The haunted house : a collection of original stories / edited by Jane Yolen and Martin H. Greenberg ; illustrated by Doron Ben-Ami.
p.   cm.
Contents: Somewhere a puppy cries / Mary K. Whittington — The paperdoll ghost / Anna Grossnickle Hines — Biscuits of glory / Bruce Coville — The gourmet ghost / Janet Gill-Lonergan — And the lights flickered/ Barbara Diamond Goldin — Night wolves / Jane Yolen — The train room / Gary Hines.
ISBN 0-06-024467-4. — ISBN 0-06-024468-2 (lib. bdg.)
1. Ghost stories, American.   2. Children's stories, American.   [1. Ghosts—Fiction.
2. Haunted houses—Fiction.   3. Short stories.]   I. Yolen, Jane.
II. Greenberg, Martin Harry.   III. Ben-Ami, Doron, ill.
PZ5.H316   1995   94-25136
[Fic]—dc20   CIP
                                                                            AC
Typography by Al Cetta
4   5   6   7   8   9   10
❖

CONTENTS

COME IN ... IF YOU DARE....

There's always a house in town that every-one agrees is haunted. But not everyone agrees on the kind of haunting that goes on there.

Maybe there are creaks and groans on the stairs. But every house has its creaks and groans.

Maybe there are lights that blink on and off and on. But couldn't there be a short circuit somewhere?

Maybe things disappear from this room or that. But maybe you just forgot where you really put them.

Whatever excuses the grown-ups find, the children always know. The house is haunted. Each new family that moves into the haunted house discovers a new kind of ghost.

One such house is 66 Brown's End, a house sometimes called The Close. And these are the stories that have been told about it. Come in . . . if you dare. . . .

When Lyssa and her mother and father and cat, Calico, moved into the house on Brown's End, only Lyssa heard the strange crying in the night—

in the cellar.

SOMEWHERE A PUPPY CRIES

MARY K. WHITTINGTON

Shivering, I hide beneath my blankets. If Calico the Cat were here, I wouldn't mind the shadows by the door, the one that won't stay closed.

"You'll be fine, Lyssa," Daddy says as he tucks me in.

"We'll be right down the hall." Mama shuts my door, but pretty soon it swings open.

That's when I hear a puppy crying. He sounds lonely. I know how he feels. Calico the Cat won't come upstairs.

Daddy says she needs to get used to this broken-down house we've just moved into. When we opened her traveling cage, she ran out to explore. But she wouldn't come when I called, not even for her dinner. At bedtime I found her by the inside cellar door, her nose

3

pressed to the bottom crack. When I tried to pick her up, she wriggled free.

My bed is so cold. I miss Calico. She always keeps me warm at night.

Every time I wake up, I hear the puppy crying. Who could he belong to? Mama says the nearest house is two miles away.

In the morning Calico still won't leave the cellar door. I give her a bowl of food, but she hardly touches it.

"She probably smells mice," Mama says at breakfast. "This house has been empty so long, there may be whole families down there."

"Could be." Daddy is fixing pancakes. "I'll take a look when I get a chance. Have to make sure it's safe before we turn her loose." He hands me my plate.

"Did you hear that puppy crying last night?" I ask.

"A puppy?" Daddy shakes his head.

"I didn't hear anything," Mama says, picking up the newspaper.

"I sure did," I say into my orange-juice glass. "He cried all night."

"Old houses make lots of strange noises," Mama says.

"Maybe ours is haunted," Daddy says in a spooky voice.

Mama laughs. "Don't worry, Lyssa. As soon as you get used to your new room, you'll sleep through everything." She pats my arm. "I bet you heard the wind blowing through a crack. That might sound like a dog whining."

I pour syrup on my pancakes. There wasn't any wind last night.

Right after breakfast, we drive into town. At a hardware store we get cans of paint, and wallpaper with flowers on it. Afterward, we go to the market. I buy two boxes of Calico's favorite kitty treats.

When we get back to the house, I stay outside for a while. "Here, pup," I call, softly because I don't want Mama or Daddy to hear. I peek under the big bushes growing around the house, but I don't find anything, not even footprints.

Inside, I give Calico a handful of treats. She purrs as she eats, but she still won't leave the cellar door.

I find Daddy and Mama peeling wallpaper off the walls in the room they call the parlor.

"Daddy," I ask, "couldn't you see if the cellar's safe now?"

"Sorry, Lyss," he says. "These walls have to be ready tonight so we can start painting. But you tell Calico I'll check it out before breakfast tomorrow, never fear."

Tonight it's colder than ever, and bright moonlight shines across my floor. Soon after I go to bed, the puppy begins to cry. I snuggle under my blankets, but I can't sleep. Suddenly, I sit up. He sounds like he's downstairs. What if he got shut up in the cellar before we moved in, and only Calico knows? It's strange, though, that I've only heard him at night. Maybe he sleeps all day.

Daddy will find him in the morning. But that doesn't make me feel any better. The pup sounds so lonely. I guess I'd better go down and get him.

Before I can change my mind, I climb out of bed. The wood floor is cold under my feet, and it creaks a little as I tiptoe into the hall. Now the puppy is howling. As I pass my parents' room, I wonder why he doesn't wake them up. Down the stairs I go and along the hallway to the kitchen. Everywhere are scary shadows, but I try not to look at them.

When Calico sees me, she stands up, stretches, and meows, as if she knows what I'm doing. The doorknob feels like ice against my hand. I wait for a moment. What if the cellar *isn't* safe? But I can't think about that now. I have to help the pup.

I tug the door open.

The howling stops.

Calico brushes past me and runs down the steps.

"Be careful," I tell her. My whisper sounds echoey.

I can't find a light switch. But there must be a window in the cellar because I see some moonlight down there. I start down the steps, feeling my way with my toes. The cellar air moves up to meet me. It smells musty and old, like no one ever comes here.

Squinting, I look among the piles of boxes against the walls. Thick dust is everywhere. It makes me sneeze.

"Where are you, pup?" I whisper. "Don't be afraid."

Something rubs against my leg. I jump, but

it's only Calico. She sits beside me, her ears pricked forward, and stares into the one corner I haven't checked.

"Meow," she says softly.

She's right. Something's there. "Puppy?"

The moonlight isn't as bright here, but I see a small dog bowl. I pick it up and brush away the dust. "Toby" it says on the side.

I wonder if this bowl belongs to the pup I've been hearing. Except he hasn't used it in a long time. *Wait a minute,* I think. Could the last owners have left him here when they moved out? But he would have starved to death. And that would mean . . .

I make myself look further into the corner. There's something bunched up—like an old blanket. And right where Calico is standing, I see a little mound. I touch it and snatch my hand back. Bones.

Daddy's right. Our house *is* haunted.

Just as my neck starts feeling prickly, I hear a sharp sound at the top of the cellar steps. *Oh no,* I think, almost forgetting the puppy as I run up to the door. It's shut. I know I left it open. For a second, I panic. But then I find the knob, turn it, and push the door open.

Probably it's like the one to my bedroom,

only this door keeps closing. Maybe that's how the pup got locked in the cellar. And his owners didn't think to look for him down there before they left. This makes me sad.

I'd better go back to bed. "Calico," I call down the steps, but she doesn't come. I use her bowl to prop open the door, knowing I'll have to tell Daddy the whole story in the morning.

Upstairs, I crawl back under the blankets. The house is quiet. Suddenly, Calico jumps up next to me. I reach out to hug her. And that's when I hear a sound coming up the hall—a clicking, like a puppy running along the floor.

"Meow," Calico says and begins to purr.

The clicking stops outside, then comes in through the shadows by the door. Something tugs at my blanket, climbs on my bed. I hear a faint whuffly noise, and Calico purrs louder.

Probably I should be scared, but I'm not. "Hi, Toby," I say. Even though the moonlight shines across my bed, I can't see him. But I hear a tail thumping against the blanket, and when I reach toward the sound, I feel a small tongue lick my hand. A little body curls up next to my feet, and Calico the Cat settles down against my back.

All night they keep me warm.

After Lyssa and her family moved out,
Kelly Conners and her family moved in.
This time the ghost is not in the cellar;

it's in the living room.

THE PAPER DOLL GHOST

ANNA GROSSNICKLE HINES

"This is your room, Ruthie," Kelly Conners said, placing a paper doll into a maroon rectangle on the old Persian rug. "And this room is for Edward."

The living room rug was the only thing the previous tenants had left in the house. At least, it was the only thing Kelly and her parents could see at first.

"That ugly thing has to go," her dad had said.

"It is awfully dreary-looking," her mother agreed, "but I'm afraid it'll have to do for a while." So she'd rolled it back and swept the musty dirt from under it.

That's when Kelly found the paper dolls. They were in an old envelope in the corner, just under the edge of the carpet.

Now the Conners family was all moved in, and Kelly, hunkered under the game table in the corner, hoped her parents would keep the old rug for a good long while. Ugly or not, it was perfect for paper dolls. The rectangles in its pattern made great rooms.

Kelly only wished she had someone to play with. School would start in two days. She wondered if the kids would like her, or if they already had all the friends they wanted.

Carefully, she folded the tabs of a yellow shirt around Edward's shoulders. "There you go," she said. "All ready for school." She picked up the red dress for Ruthie.

"Nooooo." A low moaning sound gave Kelly a shivery feeling at the back of her neck. She looked around the empty room. "Nooooooo." The moan was louder this time. "Ruuuthie wants the bluuue one."

Bonk! Kelly jerked, hitting her head on the table leg. "Ow!" she cried.

"Sooorryy," the voice moaned. "Dooon't be scaaared."

Creepy feelings ran up and down Kelly's back, making her shiver. "Wh-wh-who are you?" she stammered.

"Ooonly meeeeee." The voice seemed to be

coming from the floor in front of her, where the paper dolls lay.

Kelly picked them up, peering at their printed faces. She turned them over. There were the names she'd seen before, Ruthie and Edward, written in a shaky cursive a lot like her own. The paper dolls were old, but ordinary. They couldn't be talking. Or could they? Kelly put them down. They stared up at her.

"Who is me?" she asked.

"III aaammmm."

"Aaah!" Kelly clasped a hand to her mouth to stop the scream. The dolls hadn't moved, but in front of her a glowing figure slowly slipped out from under the rug, over the bit of bare floor and up the wall. As the figure rose, Kelly backed out from under the table and stood to face the ghostly image.

It looked like a girl, a sad girl with wispy hair and lonely eyes, but not a real girl. More like a picture of a girl projected onto the wall. Kelly looked behind her, but there was no projector, no bright light to make the image.

She turned back to see the glowing figure step first with one flat leg, then the other, away from the wall. Now that she stood in the air, Kelly could see right through her.

"Wh-who are you?"

"Estherrrr," the ghostly girl answered.

"Do you have to talk so—so spooky like that?"

"It's just been so looong since I uuused my voice." Esther bent down to pick up Ruthie and Edward in hands thinner than tissue.

"Why are you like that?" Kelly asked.

"Like whaat?"

"So thin. I can see through you."

"I'm a ghoost."

"And you're flat, like a paper doll, but without the paper. Are ghosts always flat?"

"Nooo, but I've been under the ruug."

"Why?"

"Thaat's where Aunt Myrtle left me. She always swept things that bothered her uunder the rug and she said I was a terrible bother." Esther looked at the floor.

Kelly picked up the paper clothes and held them out. "I'm sorry about these. I didn't know they belonged to someone."

Esther brightened and her voice became clear. "It's all right. Really, I don't mind. Can we play together? Please?"

Kelly hesitated. She wanted someone to play with, but not a creepy ghost. She wanted a *real* friend. Finally, not knowing what else to do, she nodded.

It was just a tiny nod, but Esther saw it. "Here," she said, "you play Ruthie and I'll take Edward."

Kelly took the paper doll and followed the ghost to her place under the table.

"Isn't this rug just the best for paper dolls?" Esther said. "Which square is the living room?"

"This green one," Kelly answered. "The blue one is Edward's bedroom."

It seemed only moments later that a voice called from the kitchen, "Kelly, supper in five minutes."

"I can't believe it's that late," Kelly remarked. "It seems like we just started."

"I know," Esther agreed. "It's been fun."

"For me, too," said Kelly, surprised at the thought.

"That's your mother in the kitchen, isn't it?" Esther asked.

Kelly nodded.

Esther looked wistful. "I wish I could see *my* mother."

"Where is she?" Kelly asked.

"In the fifth dimension, where ghosts are supposed to be."

"Can't you go there?"

"No," Esther said. "I'm only two-dimensional. You know, flat."

"Oh," Kelly said, though she didn't really understand. "Can you come back tomorrow so we can play again?"

"I can't go anyplace else," Esther said, then smiled and disappeared under the rug.

The next morning, Kelly dashed to the living room, eager to see if Esther would really be there. "Esther?" she called softly. "Esther, I'm here."

Sure enough, the image slipped out from under the rug. They grinned at one another.

"You look . . . different," Kelly said. "You have a little nose." She reached out her hand, but jerked it back when it went right through the ghost. "Oh! Does that hurt?"

"I can't even feel it." Esther giggled.

"Do you think you could ever be real again?" Kelly asked.

"I think dead is dead," Esther said. "Why?"

"I wish you could be my *real* friend, then you could go to school with me tomorrow."

"I can't do that," said Esther, "but I can play with you now."

The girl and ghost were busily doing just that when they heard footsteps coming. Esther moved quickly to slide under the rug, but her toes caught.

"Oh!" she exclaimed.

"Behind the sofa," Kelly suggested and Esther disappeared just as Kelly's dad came into the room.

"Are you all by yourself?" he asked.

Kelly nodded.

"There's been a lot of conversation for one little girl," he teased.

"I've been talking for my paper dolls," Kelly explained.

"Oh, I see. Well, I hope you're all having a good time." He winked as he went on to the kitchen.

Esther reappeared from behind the sofa. "Your father seems nice," she said pensively.

"Mostly," Kelly agreed. "Esther, something's happening to you. You're getting fat, kind of like the maps we made at school last year with papier-mâché."

"Oh, do you think so?" Esther exclaimed. "Do you think I'm getting three-dimensional?"

"Does that mean real?" Kelly asked.

"It means round, like you, not flat like a paper doll."

"Oh." Kelly's voice dropped. "So you'll still be a ghost."

Esther nodded. "But I'll be a round ghost."

"How did you get flat in the first place? Were you flat when you were alive?"

"No," Esther said. "My body was round, and so was my spirit at first, when I was with my mother and father. After they died I came to live with Aunt Myrtle, and I was a bother. She didn't really care about me, so my spirit got flatter and flatter, until I died. They buried my body in the cemetery, but my spirit has been trapped under the rug."

"You sound happy to be getting three-dimensional," Kelly said.

"Oh, I am! Very happy."

"Even if it means you can't get back under the rug?"

"I won't need to stay under the rug. If I'm three-dimensional I can go through the fourth dimension—that's time—and into the fifth dimension, where I can be with my mother and father forever."

"I don't want you to go!" Kelly cried. "You're the only friend I have here."

"You're going to school tomorrow," Esther said. "You'll make new friends there."

"What if I don't? What if none of them like to play paper dolls? What if they don't like me?"

"Oh, Kelly, they'll like you, just as I do." Esther wrapped an arm around her.

Kelly felt a sensation of coolness then warmth around her shoulders. "I like you too, Esther."

"I know. I think that's why my spirit is getting rounder."

"But if you go away, we can't play anymore."

"I'll miss that," Esther said, "but I miss my parents more. It's been so long."

Kelly tried to imagine never seeing her parents again. It was a terrible thought. Then she thought about never seeing Esther again. She didn't like that idea either. "I already miss my friends where I used to live," she whispered. "I don't want to have to miss you, too."

"It's okay," Esther said. "I'm not all round yet. Let's play some more."

So they did, laughing and chattering, dancing the dolls all about, until suddenly, Kelly stopped. She stared for a moment at Esther's arm, then followed it up to her face.

"What's the matter?" Esther asked.

"You're completely round," Kelly said.

Esther raised her arm and rotated it, examining all sides.

"You can go now." Kelly picked at the dirt under her thumbnail. Esther watched silently. Kelly thought again about never seeing her parents, then looked up. "It's okay. I'll miss you, but I'm glad for you."

Esther smiled and gathered up the paper dolls. She put them into her friend's hands. "These are really yours now."

"I'll take good care of them," Kelly said. "They'll make me think of you."

"You can use them with your new friends."

Kelly nodded. She couldn't trust her voice to say anything more.

"I'm going now," Esther said, "but I'll always think of you, Kelly. Thank you for caring about me." As she spoke her ghostly image faded away.

Only when it was completely gone did Kelly whisper softly, "Good-bye, Esther. Thank you for caring about me, too."

She scooted back under the table and spread the paper dolls on the old rug. Carefully, she folded the paper tabs around Ruthie's shoulders. "Yes, Ruthie," she said, "I do think this blue dress is best."

Benjie Perkins was just ten when he moved into The Close. His parents didn't see the ghost, but Benjie did, and this time it was

in the kitchen.

BISCUITS OF GLORY

BRUCE COVILLE

I am haunted by biscuits; Elvira Thistledown's biscuits, to be more precise. But I don't have any regrets. If I had it to do over again, I would still eat one, if only to free that poor woman from her curse. I'd do it even knowing how it was going to affect the rest of my life.

I was ten when it happened. We had just moved into a new house. Well, it was new to us; it was really a very old one—the fifth we had been in that I could remember. That was how my parents made their living: buying old houses, fixing them up, then selling them for a bundle of money. It was sort of neat, except it meant we never stayed in any one place too long, the places we moved into were always sort of crummy, and just when they got good, we had to move on.

Anyway, on our third night in the house I heard a clatter in the kitchen. Now all old houses have their noises, their own personal creaks and groans, and I was still getting used to the sounds of this house. But something about this particular noise didn't sound right to me. So I grabbed my baseball bat and headed for the stairs.

I grabbed the bat instead of waking my parents because I had been through this before. I was tired of embarrassing myself, so I generally investigated night noises on my own. But I always carried my trusty Louisville Slugger when I did. Just in case, you know?

The floor was cold against my feet.

My door squeaked as I opened it.

Trying not to wake my parents, I tiptoed along the hall, past the peeling wallpaper (roses the size of cabbages, floating against gray stripes—truly ugly), past the bathroom with its leaky faucets (I had already gotten used to *that* noise), on to the head of the stairs.

I paused and listened.

Something was definitely moving in the

kitchen. I could hear scrapes and thumps, soft and gentle, but no less real for all that. I was about to go wake my parents after all, when I heard something else—something totally unexpected.

I heard a woman singing.

I leaned forward and closed my eyes (I don't know what good that was supposed to do, but you know how it is), straining to hear. The voice was soft, sweet, and sad—almost like someone singing a hymn. I had to go halfway down the steps to make out the words:

"Biscuits, biscuits of glory
This is my story,
Biscuits of glory . . ."

By now the hair was standing up on the back of my neck. Yet somehow I didn't think anyone who sounded so sad and sweet could hurt me.

Clutching my Louisville Slugger, I tiptoed down the rest of the steps and stopped outside the kitchen door.

"Biscuits, biscuits of glory," sang the voice, sounding so sad I almost started to cry myself.

Pushing lightly on the kitchen door, I swung it open just a crack. When I peeked through, I let out a little squeak of fright. There was no one in sight, not a person to be seen.

What I did see was a bag of flour, which wouldn't have been that unusual, except for the fact that this bag was floating in mid-air.

"Biscuits of glory," sang the voice, as the bag of flour opened, seemingly by itself. "Lighter than lovin', floatin' to heaven, straight from my oven . . ."

Now a measuring cup drifted through the air and dipped into the flour bag. A little thrill ran down my spine as the cup came out of the bag. Suddenly I could see the hand that was holding it. That was because the hand was now covered with flour.

The hand repeated the action. It was an eerie sight: a floating hand, seemingly unattached to anything else, dumping flour into a big ceramic bowl.

Next came the baking powder. *Lots* of baking powder.

"Biscuits, biscuits of glory . . ." sang the ghost. Her voice caught as she choked back a sob.

I couldn't help myself. Stepping through the door into the kitchen I asked, "What is it? What's wrong?"

The flour-covered hand jerked sideways,

knocking over the container of baking powder. "Who are you?" asked the ghost in a soft voice, almost as if *she* were frightened of *me.*

"I'm Benjie Perkins. I live here. Who are you?"

"Elvira Thistledown," whispered the voice, so lightly it was as if the words were floating. "I died here."

I shivered. "What are you doing?" I asked.

"Making biscuits," she replied, setting the baking powder upright once more. "I make biscuits every Saturday night. Saturday at midnight. It's my curse."

"Sort of a strange curse."

"It was a strange death," whispered the ghost of Elvira Thistledown, as her one visible hand picked up a fork and began to stir the flour.

"Care to talk about it?" I asked.

My mother had always said I was a good listener.

"I can talk while I work," she said.

Taking that to be a yes, I pulled up a stool and sat next to the counter. Soon I was so involved in her story, I stopped paying much attention to what she was doing. Oh, how I wish now that I had watched more carefully!

"I always loved to make biscuits," said Elvira

Thistledown. "My mother taught me when I was only seven years old, and soon my daddy was saying that he thought I was the best biscuit maker in the county."

"You must have liked that."

"I did," she said, sounding happy for the first time since we had begun to talk.

"I hate to interrupt," I said, "but is it possible for you to become visible? I might feel less nervous if you did."

"Well, it's not easy. But you seem like a nice boy. Just a minute and I'll see what I can do."

Soon a milky light began to glow in front of me. It started out kind of blobby, almost like a cloud that had floated into the kitchen, but after a minute or two it condensed into the form of a woman. She was younger and prettier than I had expected, with a turned-up nose and a long neck. I don't know what color her hair or eyes were; she had no color. She wore old-fashioned clothes.

"Better?"

"I think so."

She returned to her work. "It was vanity did me in," she said, measuring baking powder into the mix. "I was so proud of my biscuits that I just couldn't stand it when that awful Dan

McCarty moved into town and started bragging that *he* made the best biscuits in the state. 'Why, my biscuits are lighter than dandelion fluff,' he used to say. 'Apt to float away on the first stiff breeze.' After a while his proud talk got to me, and I challenged him to a contest."

"What kind of a contest?"

"A biscuit bake-off," she said, dumping milk into the bowl. I realized with a start that I had no idea where she was getting her ingredients from. "Both of us to make biscuits, results to be judged by Reverend Zephyr of the Baptist Church."

"Did you win?"

She was busy working on her biscuits, so she didn't answer right away. She had turned the dough out onto the counter and was kneading it lightly. After a few minutes she began to pat it out to an even thickness. When it was about a half an inch thick she turned to me and said in a bitter voice, "I lost. I lost, and that was the beginning of my downfall. I became obsessed with biscuits. I swore I would make a better biscuit than Dan McCarty or die trying."

Using the top of the baking powder can, she began to cut the dough into rounds, flipping them off the counter and onto a baking sheet as she spoke.

"We began to have a weekly contest, Dan and I. Every Sunday morning we'd take our biscuits to church, and after the service Reverend Zephyr would try them out. He'd measure them. He'd weigh them. Finally he'd taste them, first plain, then with butter, then with honey. And every Sunday he'd turn to me and say, 'I'm sorry, Elvira, but Dan's biscuits are just lighter and fluffier than yours.' "

She popped the tray into the oven. "I was like a madwoman. I worked day and night, night and day, trying every combination I could think of to make my biscuits lighter, fluffier, more wonderful than any that had ever been made. I wanted biscuits that would float out of the oven and melt in your mouth. I wanted biscuits that would make a kiss seem heavy. I wanted biscuits that would make the angels weep with envy. I tried adding whipped egg whites, baking soda and vinegar, even yeast. But do too much of that, and you don't really have a biscuit anymore. No, the key is in the baking powder."

Her eyes were getting wild now, and I was beginning to be frightened again. I wondered if she really was crazy—and if she was, just what a crazy ghost might do.

"One Sunday I was sure I had it; I came to church with a basket of biscuits that were like a stack of tiny featherbeds. But after the judging Reverend Zephyr shook his head sadly and said, 'I'm sorry, Elvira, but Dan's biscuits are just lighter and fluffier than yours.'

"By the next Saturday night I was wild, desperate, half insane. In a fit of desperation, I dumped an entire can of baking powder into my dough."

"What happened?" I asked breathlessly.

"The oven door blew off and killed me on the spot. And ever since, I've been doomed to bake a batch of biscuits every Saturday at midnight, as punishment for my pride. What's worse, I finally know the secret. Learned it on the other side. These biscuits are the lightest, fluffiest ever made, Benjie. Just plain heavenly. But no one has ever tasted them. And I can't rest until someone does."

"How come no one has ever tasted them?"

"How can they? My biscuits of glory are so light and fluffy they float right out of the oven and disappear through the ceiling. If I could leave them on the counter overnight, someone might have tried them by now. But they're always gone before anyone gets a chance." She sounded like she was going to cry. "I'm so weary of biscuits," she sighed, "so everlastingly weary of baking biscuits."

"These biscuits of yours—they wouldn't hurt someone who ate them, would they?"

"Of course not!" she cried, and I could tell that I had offended her. "These are Biscuits of Glory. One bite and you'll never be the same."

"What if I grabbed one as it came out of the oven?"

"You'd burn your hand."

"Wait here!" I said.

Scooting out of the kitchen, I scurried up the stairs and rummaged through my room until I found what I was looking for—not easy, when you've just moved. When I finally I located it I went down the stairs two at a time, hoping to make it to the kitchen before Elvira's biscuits came out of the oven.

She was standing by the big old oven as I slipped through the swinging door.

"What's that?" she asked, as I came in.

"My catcher's mitt. Are the biscuits ready?"

"They can't wait any longer," she replied. "They're done to perfection."

As she spoke, she opened the oven door. Out floated a dozen of the most perfect biscuits I had ever seen—light, golden brown, high and fluffy, crusty around the edges. They escaped in sets of three, rising like hot air balloons at the state fair.

Reaching out with the mitt, I snagged a biscuit from the third set.

"Careful," said Elvira. "They're hot!"

Ignoring her warning, I took the biscuit from the glove. "Ow!" I cried as it slipped through my fingers and headed for the ceiling.

The last row of biscuits had already left the oven. I scrambled onto the counter and snagged one just as it was heading out of reach. I was more careful this time, cupping the glove over it and holding it tenderly while it cooled. I could feel the heat, but the leather protected me.

Finally I thought it was safe to try a bite. Elvira Thistledown watched with wide eyes as I took her work from my glove and lifted it to my lips.

It was astonishing, the most incredible biscuit I had ever tasted.

Suddenly I realized something even more astonishing: *I* was floating! I had lifted right off the counter and was hovering in midair. I worried about getting down, but as I chewed and swallowed, I drifted gently to the floor.

"What an amazing biscuit," I cried. "I feel like I've died and gone to heaven!"

"So do I!" said Elvira Thistledown. Only the last word was dragged out into an eyeeeeeeee . . ., as if she were being snatched into the sky.

That was the last I ever saw of Elvira Thistledown.

Her biscuits, however, haunt me still. It's not just the memory of their taste, though I have never again tasted anything so fine. It's the effect of the darned things. See, whenever I get too happy, or too excited, or begin thinking about those biscuits too much, I start to float. If I dream of them—and I often do—I may wake to find myself drifting a foot or two above the bed.

It gets a little embarrassing sometimes.

I'll tell you this, though. Unlike some people, I'm not afraid of what happens after you die.

I know what I'll find waiting on the other side.

. . . Biscuits of Glory.

Mark and his little sister, Sally, knew about the hungry ghost, even though their mother did not. It was a ghost that haunted

the dining room.

THE GOURMET GHOST

JANET E. GILL

My mom handed me a plate of pancakes. "Go eat with your sister in the dining room, Mark."

I drowned them in syrup. "Dining room?" I didn't like that room.

"Sally insisted on eating there. Something about an imaginary friend." Mom shrugged. "Ahber, I think she called him."

I started for the room.

"Some women are coming by to see the furniture I'm selling," Mom went on. "Mrs. Carr from down the street and later, Mrs. Glades and her son. Said he goes to your school."

My heart flip-flopped. Ricky Glades, meanest kid in the whole school. Last week, he stole my three best baseball cards. Yesterday, he followed my friend and me home, calling us names all the way. And he was coming here. I'd better hide out.

I shivered as I stepped into the dining room. It was always cold. And dark, because of the heavy curtains. My sister was sitting on the hardwood floor, a plate of pancakes before her. We'd just moved into this house. Lots of old furniture came with it, but no dining room table.

I started to sit by Sally.

"No, Mark!" she said. "Ahber dair."

The invisible friend. I sat across from her. "You're silly."

She gave me the smile everyone calls angelic. Her blond curls just add to the look. Mom told me even my blond hair couldn't make me look like an angel.

"Ahber hungee, Mark," Sally said. "Ahber eat." She waved her fork with a piece of pancake on it.

The pancake disappeared!

"How'd you do that?" I asked.

"Ahber hungee. Ahber eat."

Feeling dumb, I held out a pancake. Cold air rushed past my hand, then, no pancake. My scalp prickled.

"Ahber eat!" Giggling, Sally bounced up and down.

I tossed an orange wedge. The fruit vanished.

Another. Gone, too. Squealing with excitement, Sally threw her plate.

"No, it'll break!" I cried.

But instead of a crash, I heard a small gulp. The dish had disappeared, too.

Mom came in. "What's going on?"

"We're just talking," I said.

"Don't leave a mess. Mrs. Carr wants to see the chandelier."

I gazed up at the huge crystal chandelier. It hung, all glittery, like a frozen fountain. Mom's walking had made it sway, because the wires holding it up were weak. Since it cost a lot to get them fixed, my parents had decided to sell it.

Mom left, and I trailed Sally to the far end of the room. Arms spread wide, she leaned forward and hugged the air. She looked like she should tip over, but she didn't.

"Ahber go night-night." She patted the floor in the corner.

"What's he look like?" I asked.

Stretching her arms up, she stood on tiptoe. "Ahber big."

"Like Dad? Grandpa?" I wished she could talk more.

She pointed at a large, scenic painting on the wall. "Dat."

Ahber looked like a waterfall? A wide short waterfall? Like a fat ghost.

A ghost! No wonder this room was creepy. But shouldn't he be rattling chains? Making scary noises? I never heard of a ghost who ate breakfast.

Sally went into the kitchen, leaving me alone with our ghost. What if he only liked little kids? Maybe he wouldn't want me in his bedroom.

"Ahber," I whispered. "It's me, Mark. I'm the one who fed you breakfast. Remember?"

No creaks. No moans.

In case he was asleep, I tiptoed around, humming softly so he wouldn't think I was spying. Stopping at the huge chest Mom calls an armoire, I slid the drawers out, in, out, in. One stuck, and I worked it open. Crumpled inside was a white apron big enough to wrap a large Humpty Dumpty. Red initials on it said A. A. As I held it up, a piece of paper drifted out. On it was a photograph of a man. His cheeks were so fat, they looked as though he'd puffed them out. Three chins hid his neck. Beside the picture it said

Albert Anders died suddenly Tuesday.
Anders, a gourmet, spent his life
searching for the perfect meal. He

stated he was always hungry and always
had room for one more bite. His death
occurred during a dinner party at his home.
Anders leaves no family.

Albert. Ahber in baby talk. And he'd died here, in this room. I shuffled my feet. I could be standing on the exact spot.

Was he hanging around waiting for that perfect meal? Well, Mom's cooking was all right, but not gourmet.

The doorbell rang.

"It's Mrs. Carr," Mom said. She brought my sister into the room. I shoved the apron and paper back. Sally headed for the corner where we'd left Ahber.

Voices sounded in the kitchen, then a dog yipped.

Tap, tap, tap. The dog trotted into the dining room. I knew this dog. It always nipped at me when I rode my bike. Yesterday, I had to kick it away. The dog remembered, too. Eyes on me, it crouched, growling. I stepped back.

"Goggy!" Sally rushed toward it.

The dog leaped at her—and then, it vanished. Just disappeared, as though it had never been. The gulp this time was loud.

Sally laughed. "Bye-bye, Goggy. Ahber hungee."

Chills ran down my back as I stared at the nothing beside me. Was that dog Ahber's idea of the perfect meal?

"The chandelier's in here." Mom led a large woman in.

She looked up, then around. "Where's my dog?" she asked.

"He wanted to go out," I told her.

Her face turned red. "How could you have done that? He'll get lost!" She stomped from the room, Mom following.

Tinkle. Tinkle, tinkle. The footsteps had set the chandelier swinging. My eyes tracked it back and forth. The sound, growing louder, was like a flock of twittering birds.

Snap! Crack! Snap!

The chandelier dropped, right at Sally and me. Grabbing her hand, I rushed for the door.

GULP!

The chandelier disappeared.

Sally looked up, her eyes big. "Ahber berry hungee, Mark."

A chandelier! A whole giant chandelier. A dog. A plate. This ghost would eat anything!

Before I could think of how to explain this

to my mom, another woman's voice came from the kitchen. "I'm interested in your four-poster bed."

"Fine," Mom said. "Your son can wait in the dining room with my children."

Then, Ricky Glades, looking as big and mean as ever, stood in the doorway. I'd forgotten he was coming! He planted himself right in front of me. My hands clenched.

"Little Markie having fun with his baby sister," he sneered.

Eat anything, I suddenly thought. *Always hungry.*

Ricky's red face came so close I could count his eyelashes. One finger jabbed my shoulder. "Sissy." Jab. "Weirdo." Jab. "Little bitty weeny." Jab, jab.

And always room for one more bite.

I raised my fists. "Bug off, creep."

His mouth dropped open. Then, he charged. I waited for Ahber to react. Instead, Ricky piled into me and punched me hard on the nose.

"Sally, where's Ahber?" I cried, holding my nose.

"Oh, Mark," she said. "Ahber not hungee anymore."

Jason's mother and father never believed in the ghost. Neither did the sitter, Mrs. Williford. But Jason's friend Toby, who told the ghost stories, believed that there was a ghost

in the bathroom.

AND THE LIGHTS FLICKERED

BARBARA DIAMOND GOLDIN

Jason kissed his mom and dad good-bye. "Now, remember," said his mother. "Mrs. Williford next door will be checking in on you. Go to her if you have any problems."

"I will," said Jason, though he had no intention of going over there. Not to nosy old Mrs. Williford's. He just wanted his parents to get going already.

"And don't pay any attention to that friend of yours, Toby, and his stories about the house being haunted," said his dad. "The house is old and there are lots of settling noises."

"I'm not worried, Dad. Anyway, you're only going to be gone for a few hours. And there's always Mrs. Williford." What good she would be in an emergency, Jason couldn't imagine, but it seemed to make his parents feel better knowing she was there.

Jason waved to his mom and dad through the living room window as they finally drove away.

"Yeah!" he shouted when their car disappeared down the street. It was the first time they'd ever left him alone. Well almost, except for Mrs. Williford.

He grabbed the chips and a soda and sat down in front of the TV.

He munched on the chips. Drank some soda. Watched the cartoons.

When he looked at his watch, an hour had gone by. Where was Mrs. Williford?

Jason smiled. *She's probably fallen asleep and forgotten all about me,* he thought. That would be just like her. He relaxed. Now he could *really* do what he wanted. He got some cookies. The kind with the cream in the middle. And then he played with his new video game, Battle Ants.

Wish Toby was here, he thought. But his parents wouldn't let him have Toby over while they were gone.

Thinking of Toby made Jason shudder. Toby and his haunted house stories! Trying to scare him at that last sleepover. Jason had been up all night listening to every *creak* in the house after that story about the ghost hand. The hand without a body that got you in the night.

Jason looked at his watch again. An hour and a half. Mrs. Williford had definitely forgotten about him. This time he didn't smile. He was almost sorry Caroline, his regular sitter, wasn't there.

But no. Jason had argued with his parents: "I'm getting too old for sitters. It's during the day and there's nothing to be scared of."

Well, there isn't, is there? Jason thought.

He sat on the living room rug in front of the TV and noticed, suddenly, how quiet it was in the house. Except for the video game. And how dark. It had gotten cloudy, stormy outside. Then Jason realized: He had to go to the bathroom.

Wish there was a bathroom down here, he thought. But there wasn't.

He looked up the stairs. It was dark and creepy up there. All he could think of was that hand.

He got up and put the lights on. Every light. The living room. The dining room. The kitchen. Toby said that ghosts don't like light. Not that he believed Toby, of course. But . . .

He walked back to the stairs. Now it was light at the bottom. But still very dark at the top. Reluctantly, he started up the stairs.

With each step, there was a loud *creeak*.

He kept going. Finally, he was at the top. He could see the bathroom. But, funny thing: The door was closed. The door was never closed unless someone was in there. Was someone in there? Or something? Jason shuddered.

Oh, you're just a scaredy cat, he told himself.

He reached out for the door.

Just then, there was a strange, high whistling sound. A wail.

Eeee. Eeee. Eeee.

It came from the bathroom.

Jason stood there with his hand straight out. He didn't budge.

Then the lights down below, the ones he'd put on, flickered. On and off. On and off.

And the wail came again.

Eeee. Eeee. Eeee.

This time Jason did budge. He turned around and ran down the stairs and out the front door so fast that Mr. Nolan, the gym teacher, wouldn't have believed it.

But he didn't run to Mrs. Williford's house.

He ran to Toby's. Toby knew all about this kind of thing.

"Toby! Toby! A ghost!" he shouted as he neared Toby's yard.

Toby wasn't out in the yard, so Jason knocked on the door.

Mrs. Elias, Toby's mother, answered. Jason took a deep breath. "Is Toby here?" he said.

"Why, no. Isn't he over at your house? He left about twenty minutes ago," she said. "That boy. Now where is he?"

"At my house?" Jason muttered. "How could he be at my house?"

Then he understood. *So that's Toby's game,* he thought. *Trying to scare me. Boy, will I get him.*

"You're right," Jason said out loud to Mrs. Elias. "He is at my house. I forgot. In the bathroom. I'll go right back there. Thanks. See ya."

Mrs. Elias stood there, looking totally confused, as Jason went down the walk back toward his house. He tried to come up with a plan to scare Toby. It wasn't so easy. Even now, Jason couldn't figure out how Toby had snuck into his house. Or how he had shut the lights on and off if he was in the bathroom.

When he passed Mrs. Williford's house, she called out to him from the front door.

"Jason, I was worried about you," she said, her head bobbing up and down as it always did. "I'm sorry. I fell asleep for a little while. But when I woke up, I went over to check on you and you weren't there! The TV was on and the door was wide open and—"

"Oh, don't worry, Mrs. Williford. I had to tell Toby something. I'm fine. Everything's fine. No problems."

"Just don't come in. Just don't come in," Jason repeated under his breath. Mrs. Williford didn't. She went back inside.

Jason got to his front door and crept in quietly, hoping Toby was still in the bathroom. He shut all the lights off, one by one. Luckily, it was still cloudy and dark outside. And luckily, he knew where his mom kept the Halloween stuff, the tape with the cackling noises and the crazy laughing and whooshing sounds.

He carried the tape recorder and tape up the stairs and let the steps creak slowly, one by one, as he made his way up.

He knew Toby would be pretty scared himself by now, being in that bathroom all alone for so long. Jason hoped Toby hadn't snuck out while he was gone.

Jason plugged in the tape recorder and smiled.

Creepy noises filled the house.

Hee. Hee. Hee. Oooooo.

Suddenly the bathroom door swung open. His friend Toby flew out and down the stairs. His face had the look of someone who had just woken up in the middle of a graveyard.

Jason ran after him and caught up with him right outside the front door. Mr. Nolan would have been proud of Toby, too.

Jason grabbed Toby by the shoulders.

"Some friend you are," he said, grinning.

"Some friend *you* are," Toby said back.

They both started laughing.

"Boy, were you scared!" Toby said.

"Boy, were *you* scared!" Jason said. "Hey, I forgot. I still have to go to the bathroom. Let's go back inside."

Jason reached for the doorknob. "You know, Toby, I never figured out how you crept past me."

"Easy. I just climbed up that tree outside your bedroom window and let myself in."

"And how did you get those lights to flicker like that?"

"What lights are you talking about?"

"Oh, stop teasing me," said Jason.

Just then Jason noticed the lights in the house. Funny. They were on again. And they were flickering. On and off. On and off.

He poked Toby. They both looked inside. Then they saw it. It was a hand. Reaching for the curtain. No body attached. Just a hand.

Jason looked at Toby. Toby stared back at him. And without a word, they both ran for it. Down the street to Toby's as fast as they could go.

Pete already believed in night wolves and a bear in his closet when they moved into the house on Brown's End. So he wasn't really all that surprised to find a ghost

in the bedroom.

NIGHT WOLVES

JANE YOLEN

When we moved into the old house on Brown's End, I knew the night wolves would move with us. And the bear. They had lived in every bedroom I'd ever had—the one in Allentown and the one in Phoenix and the one in Westport.

The wolves lived under my bed, the bear in my closet. They only came out at night.

I knew—I *absolutely* knew—that if I got out of bed in the middle of the night, I was a goner. You couldn't begin to imagine how big that bear was or how many teeth those wolves had. *You* couldn't imagine. But I could.

So I put the bear trap I had made out of Legos and paper clips in front of the closet. And I put the wolf trap I had built out of my brother

Jensen's broken pocketknife and the old Christmas tree stand at the foot of my bed. And I kept the night-light on, even though I was ten when we moved to Brown's End.

That meant, of course, that no one dared come into my room in the dark, not Mom or Jensen, or even Dad, though we rarely saw him since he got married to Kate. And none of my friends stayed overnight.

It was safer that way.

Of course the minute it got to be light outside, the wolves and bear disappeared. I never did figure out where they went. And then I could go to the bathroom. Or get a new book from my bookcase. Or sit on the floor to put on my socks. Or anything.

Which meant winters were tough, especially now that we were living in the north, the dawn coming so late and all.

In Phoenix once, when I was eight, I was sick to my stomach and I just *had* to go to the bathroom. I waited and waited until it was almost too late, then made a dash over the foot of my bed. I managed to get out of the room in one big leap, my heart pounding so loud it sounded like I had a rock band inside. But I had to spend the rest of the night curled up in the tub because I could hear the wolves sniffing and snuffling around the bathroom door.

So when we moved to Brown's End without my dad, I expected the wolves and the bear. I just didn't expect the ghost.

I heard it on the very first night, a kind of low sobbing: *ooh-wooo-oooooooo.*

The wolves heard it, too, and it made them nervous. They rushed around under my bed, growling and scratching all night, trying to get past the trap.

The next night the bear heard it, too. He thrashed around so in the closet that when dawn came and I opened the closet door, my best sweater and my confirmation suit had fallen to the floor.

But the third night, the low sobbing turned into a cry that came from across the hall in the room where my mom slept. And then I was *really* scared.

"Mom!" I called out. I usually don't like to do that for fear of reminding the wolves and bear that I am in the room with them. Then a little louder I called out, "Mom?"

She didn't wake up and call back that everything was all right.

So then I did something I *never* do. I called

to Jensen, who was in the next room. Ever since Phoenix we've had our own rooms. I hated to do that because he always teases me anyway, calling me a baby for needing a night-light. A baby! He's only eleven himself.

But Jensen didn't wake up, either. In fact I could hear him snoring. If I could only snore like that, I bet there wouldn't be any wolves or bear around my room.

I tried to sleep, but the ghost's sobbing came again.

I put the pillow over my head but somehow that made it worse.

I stayed that way until dawn. I didn't sleep much.

"Do you suppose this house is haunted?" I asked at breakfast, before we headed off to our new school.

Jensen snorted into his cereal. But Mom put her head to one side and considered me for a long while.

"Yeah, haunted," Jensen said. "By the ghosts of wolves. And a big ugly closet bear." I had made the mistake of telling the family about them when I was littler. And back when we were a family. Dad had teased me—and so had Jensen.

"Jensen . . ." Mom warned.

So I didn't bring it up again. Not at breakfast and not at dinner, either. But when we went to bed that night, I borrowed two pieces of cotton from Mom's dresser and stuck them in my ears. Then I brushed my teeth, went to the bathroom, and jumped into bed. It's when I hit the bed the first time at night that the wolves know it's time to wake up. And the bear.

Mom came in and kissed me good night. She turned on the night-light and turned off the overhead.

"Leave the door open," I reminded her. Not that she ever needed reminding.

And I lay down and quickly fell asleep.

It was well past midnight that I woke. The wolves and bear were quiet. It was the ghost sobbing loudly in Mom's room that woke me. I was surprised it hadn't wakened her. But then she doesn't hear the wolves or bears, either. She says that since I do, I'm a hero every time I get into bed. I know I'm no hero—but I'd sure like to be.

The ghost went on and on and I began to wonder if it were dangerous. Bad enough that Dad was gone. If anything should happen to Mom . . .

I thought about that for a long time. After all, the foot of my bed was even closer to the door than it had been in Phoenix. And I was bigger.

I pulled the cotton out of my ears. The sound of the crying was so loud, the house seemed to shake with it. How could *anyone* sleep through that racket? I sat up in bed and the wolves began to growl. The bear pushed the closet door open and it squeaked a little in protest, inching out against the trap.

Ohowwwwwwwwwwwwooooooooo.

And then Mom's voice came, only terribly muffled. "Pete!" she cried. My name. And my Dad's.

Only Dad wasn't there.

That's when I knew that wolves and bear or no—I had to help her. I was her only hope.

"Get back, you suckers!" I shouted at the wolves, and threw the cotton balls down. They landed softly on the floor by the bed and muzzled the wolves.

"Leave me alone, you big overgrown rug!" I called to the bear, flinging my pillow at the closet door. The pillow thudded against the door, jamming it.

Without thinking it through any further

than that, I jumped from the bed foot and landed, running, through the door. Two steps brought me into my mom's room.

That was when I saw it—the ghost, hovering over her bed. It was all in white, a slim female ghost in a long dress and a white veil. She was crying and crying.

"Why . . ." I said, my voice shaking, "why are you here? Who are you?"

The ghost turned toward me and slowly lifted her veil. I shivered, expecting to see maybe a shining skull with dark eye sockets or a monster with weeping sores or—I don't know—maybe even a wolf's head. But what I saw was like a faded familiar photograph. It took me a moment to understand. And then I knew—the ghost wore my mother's face, my mother's wedding dress. She was young and slim and . . . beautiful.

Behind me in my room, the wolves had set up an awful racket. The bear had joined in snuffling and snorting. When I looked I could see red eyes glaring at me at the door's edge.

The ghost caught her breath and shivered.

"It's all right," I said. "They won't hurt us. Not here." I put my hand out to her. "And don't be sad. If you hadn't gotten married, where would I be? Or Jensen?"

The ghost looked at me for a long moment, considering, then lowered the veil.

"Pete? Honey?" My mom's voice came from the bed, sleepy yet full of wonder. "What are you doing in my room?"

"Being a hero, I guess," I said to her and to the wedding ghost and to myself. "You were having an awful bad dream."

"Not a bad dream, sweetie. A sad dream," she said. "And then I remembered I had you and your brother and it was all happy again. Do you want me to walk you back to your room?"

I looked over at the doorway. The red eyes were gone. "Nah," I said. "Who's afraid of a couple of night wolves and an old bear anyway? That's kid stuff." I kissed her on the cheek and watched as the ghost faded into the first rays of dawn. "I think I'm gonna like it here, Mom."

I marched back into my room and picked up the trap from the foot of my bed, then the one from in front of the closet door. I heard whimpers, like a litter of puppies, coming from under the bed. I heard a big snore from the closet. I smiled. "I'm gonna like it here a lot."

Wesley considered the house at Brown's End a mansion. At least it seemed that way when he visited his grandfather there. A mansion with a special kind of haunted tower room

in the attic.

THE TRAIN ROOM

GARY HINES

The little man stood by the window in the third-floor tower room. One eye opened slowly. He watched as a limousine let out *Wesley Hopkins. The little man did not move, which made sense. But the opening eye was truly odd. It had always been shut before. After all, it was painted on, typical for a train conductor made of wood.*

"Is my room set up, Grandpop?" Wesley asked eagerly as he walked through the door of the mansion.

"Yes," his grandfather answered.

"Hooray!" Wesley shouted.

"Do you really think you should let him get

so carried away with all this?" Wesley's father asked, coming in behind his son.

The older Mr. Hopkins stroked his chin and smiled slightly. "Oh, someday he'll learn our own actions come back to haunt us."

Wesley snatched his suitcase from his father's hand and, with a quick, "I'll see you tomorrow, Dad," dashed up the stairs to the third floor.

His room, the train room, was in one of the house's three towers. Wesley charged through the door. He clapped his hands and whooped.

The train tracks encircled the round room on a narrow table. The only opening was at the door where a drawbridge was raised to let him in.

He lowered the drawbridge, dropped his suitcase, and leaped knees first onto the bed, which sat precisely in the center of everything.

Good! he thought, noting his grandfather had replaced the two engines Wesley had wrecked during his last visit. Now there was a new red and silver Santa Fe diesel and a shiny, black steam locomotive with "Union Pacific" painted on the tender.

Wesley glanced out the window as his father's limousine drove off. "Out of the way, little man," he said, knocking the toy train conductor away from the tracks. He flicked on the electric transformer.

The Santa Fe pulled onto the main line as Wesley increased the power. Round the room it went, pulling four cars. Faster . . . faster.

Sparks flew from the caboose wheels—*Pop! Snap!*—as it bounced up and derailed, clunking to rest upside down across the track.

Wesley grinned and pushed the throttle. The locomotive whined as it tore around the room. Only its magnetic wheels kept it on the rails. Other cars came off, one at a time, until only the engine was left, screaming at full speed, bearing down on the helpless caboose. With a loud crash, the caboose careened to the floor as the sleek Santa Fe tipped over, slammed into the wall, and crunched to a stop.

"Wow! That was great!" Wesley shouted.

But across the room, facing Wesley's back, the little man slowly opened his eye once more.

Wesley slept peacefully, sprawled across his bed within the circle of track. His day had been full of wrecks.

It was late, past midnight.

And that's when it started, a faint, almost imperceptible scratching.

Scratch . . . scratch . . . (like a whisper) *scratch.*

Wesley rolled over.

Scratch . . . scratch.

Wesley lay still.

More scratching.

Wesley's eyes opened.

Had he heard something? Maybe not. He flopped on his belly.

Scratch . . . scratch . . . scratch.

There it is again.

Wesley rose up. He reached for the lamp and turned the switch. No light. Odd.

He stared into the darkness, then blinked his eyes. There, by the water tower, was a dim glow. Shaking his head, Wesley swallowed thickly and stood up, pulled toward the strange light.

It grew brighter, drawing him closer until a shape became clear. It was the little conductor, still as stone, bathed in the eerie glow. Wesley bent down.

Both the little man's eyes opened. Wesley jumped back.

The conductor raised his arm. "You!" he said.

Wesley's jaw dropped but no sound came out

as the ghostly light enveloped him.

The little man grew and grew. So did the train tracks and the trains. Wesley's skin went clammy. His eyes rolled back and forth. Everything in the room was growing.

No. He was *shrinking!*

Panicked, Wesley tried to run, but like in a dream, nothing worked: not his arms, legs, hands, feet—nothing.

The little man watched, pleased, his arm still pointing at Wesley. And when Wesley had shrunken to the conductor's size, he found himself on the tracks, standing helplessly.

The conductor's eyes grew cold and his eyebrows rose scornfully. "You wreck us, Wesley Hopkins, now we wreck you!"

A loud click spat behind Wesley. He turned, gasping. The black steam engine, gigantic and powerful, hummed to life. Its headlamp caught Wesley in its light. Then the wheels began turning, spinning on the rails as they fought for traction.

Wesley stumbled to the side, trying to get off the tracks. He yelled as a chain-link fence hit him full in the face. Where had that come from? His railroad didn't have a fence. He spun around. All along the track, on both sides, was high fencing, too high to get over.

The locomotive moved, slowly, its wheels gripping and pistons groaning. Steam hissed from its belly. It was alive now, fully awake, and coming after him. Terrified, Wesley looked at it. Taking a step back and tripping, falling, pushing himself backward, he finally scrambled to his feet.

Wide eyed, mouth open, he turned and started running. His only escape was down the tracks.

Maybe I'll find an opening in the fence, he thought. *Maybe there'll be a place low enough to climb over.*

Maybe.

The shrill whistle blew. Wesley cried out, screams pouring from his mouth. Then, somewhere, over the building noise, he heard laughter and looked up. Ahead, outside the fence, was the conductor, still pointing at Wesley and laughing.

The steam engine came closer, closer, and Wesley, running and gasping hard now, cried at every breath.

Squinting through his sweat, Wesley saw the conductor again, this time pointing down and away from him, down to the ground. But it wasn't the ground he was pointing to, it was the edge of the table, the gigantic, high train table.

Wesley stumbled up and looked into the darkness. He spun around, wailing in fright as the giant steam beast surged toward him.

The conductor called out, "Jump! Jump!" and laughed again.

The locomotive swelled to a monstrous shadow that seemed to swallow up the sky. Wesley shrieked and toppled as the engine's cow catcher forced him over the edge and into the emptiness.

Wesley woke on the floor. Next to him was the little steam engine, turned on its side. Sunlight filled the room.

He gathered himself and sat up, shaking.

I must have fallen out of bed and somehow swiped the locomotive with my arm, he thought.

Across the room, next to the window, was the toy conductor. Wesley walked over cautiously. The little man was like he'd always been, both eyes closed and a smug look painted on his face. Wesley looked at him for a moment, then smiled and sighed deeply.

His father arrived a bit later to pick him up.

"How many do I have to replace this time?" Wesley's grandfather asked, hugging him goodbye.

Wesley smiled. "Just a couple. But that'll be it. I don't think I'll be wrecking trains anymore."

"Oh?" his grandfather asked, his brow lifting.

"I think playing *regular* trains might be more fun."

Wesley's grandfather opened the door of the third-floor train room and peered in. By the window, watching a limousine drive away, stood a little man. He smiled. This was odd. But odder still was the wink he exchanged with old Mr. Hopkins. After all, his mouth and eyes were only painted on, typical for a train conductor made of wood.

ABOUT THE AUTHORS

BRUCE COVILLE is one of America's favorite children's books authors. His popular *My Teacher Is an Alien* series, as well as the *Space Brat* series and the *Magic Shop* series have earned him a large and admiring readership. He lives in Syracuse, New York.

JANET E. GILL is the author of several novels, fantasy short stories, and poems. She lives in Washington state with her three children and three cats.

BARBARA DIAMOND GOLDIN is the author of over half a dozen picture books and short novels for young readers, including the award-winning JUST ENOUGH IS PLENTY, THE WORLD'S BIRTHDAY, and the powerful book about the seder: THE PASSOVER JOURNEY. She lives in Northampton, Massachusetts.

ANNA GROSSNICKLE HINES has been called "the sorceress of the ordinary" for her wonderful realistic picture books like GRANDMA GETS GRUMPY, DADDY MAKES THE BEST SPAGHETTI, and two dozen others she has both written and illustrated. She lives in Milford, Pennsylvania.

GARY HINES is a forestry ranger who also writes children's books. He has three books published, including A RIDE ON THE CRUMMY. He lives with his wife, Anna Grossnickle Hines, in Milford, Pennsylvania.

MARY K. WHITTINGTON is a piano teacher and children's book author with almost a half dozen books to her credit, including THE PATCHWORK LADY and WINTER'S CHILD. She also teaches writing courses near her home in Kirkland, Washington.

JANE YOLEN is the author of over 150 books for children and adults, including the Caldecott winning OWL MOON, and a series of anthologies: VAMPIRES, WEREWOLVES, THINGS THAT GO BUMP IN THE NIGHT. Her children's novels and music books are also popular. She lives in Hatfield, Massachusetts.

MARTIN H. GREENBERG is possibly the best known anthologist in America today. He is also a college professor, a consultant, and has well over a hundred books to his credit. He lives in Green Bay, Wisconsin.

The haunted house.

$13.89

DATE			